To Eva
The heroine of the story!

Eva Panda and her friends are playing their best-loved game of roly poly.

It is lots of fun and much better than walking.

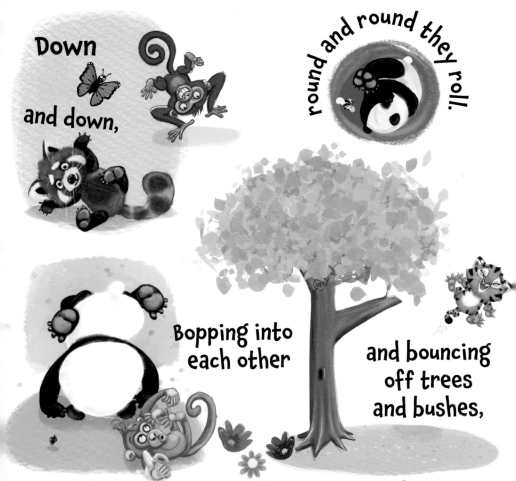

Down

and down,

round and round they roll.

Bopping into each other

and bouncing off trees and bushes,

Pandas are so fluffy they never get hurt.

Suddenly –

SPLASH

they roll into an unexpected puddle of water.
Where has it come from? It hasn't been raining!

As they shake the water from their fur,

Eva can see that the nearby river has burst its banks and she wonders why.

7

Eva looks downstream and notices
that the river is blocked with plastic
bottles and other rubbish.
"Oh no!" exclaims Eva
"the water can't get through."

8

"We will have to remove the rubbish, or more of the jungle could be flooded. That would be a disaster for our friends and food supply." says Eva.
But how?

Eva looks around and sees her friend Tumble is eating some bamboo...

...and this gives her an idea.

Eva asks Tumble to chomp down two long lengths of bamboo,

while she tears off strips from another piece and cleverly twists the strips into a net.

11

Working together the friends make an amazing makeshift bridge.

They wonder how to get it across the water.

"I know" says the tallest stretchiest monkey, waggling his floppy hands, "I can swing across!"

Using an extra long vine and taking an extra big leap...

12

...the monkey swings safely to the other side, landing like an acrobat.

Bit by bit, Eva and her friends push the bamboo bridge across to him. The monkey stretches out his long arms and grabs the bridge, then using some vines he ties the bamboo bridge tightly to a nearby tree.

Eva carefully shimmies out onto the bridge. Being a bear, she's not scared of climbing.

Just as she reaches the middle she loses her grip and starts to slip!

Luckily she manages to hang on with her strong legs and sharp claws. Dangling upside down, she sees that she is close to the rubbish swirling in the water below.

Clinging on to the bridge, Eva begins scooping up the nasty rubbish with the net.

The other jungle creatures all want to help, so Eva passes the rubbish filled net to a monkey...

...who then gives it to the red panda...

...who finally hands it to the tiger!

The tiger empties the rubbish into one big pile.
"Why don't we call ourselves the Eco Crew,
as we are doing such a good job."
says the tiger. "That is a great idea."
says **Eva**.

Finally, the last piece of rubbish is collected...

...and the river runs freely again. HOORAY!

Tumble the red panda asks where the rubbish came from.

Eva explains that instead of recycling it,

some people just throw their rubbish on the ground and a lot of it ends up in rivers and even in the SEA!

"That is terrible," says the red panda.
"We should remind everyone that -
If everybody does their bit
the planet will be fighting fit."

Eva and the Eco Crew stand in front
of the big pile of rubbish, happy with
doing their bit to help.

The end